To Sue,

Jimmy: Of Life and Lives

with Love

Delia Denver.

x

Jimmy:
Of Life and Lives

By Delia Denver

Strategic Book Group
Durham, Connecticut

Strategic Book Group
P. O. Box 333
Durham, CT 06422
http://www.strategicbookclub.com

ISBN: 978-1-61204-461-3

Book Design by Julius Kiskis

19 18 17 16 15 14 13 12 11   1 2 3 4 5

Dedication

To my darling mother and father, my beloved husband
Don, and my dear son Bob, thank you for all of your
support and patience.

Introduction

The year was 1930 and The Depression was hitting hard, with families struggling to make ends meet and failing miserably. Britain's smallest-size coin was a farthing, which was the equivalent to the American dime. There were four farthings in one penny.

Jimmy Brown, skinny and scruffy, with mousy hair, freckles, and dirt, was a typical eight-year-old, with one difference—today he would kill both of his parents and, sadly, himself as well.

One hundred and twenty-five years earlier, across the world in New York, in a place Jimmy hadn't even heard of, a young woman lived that would become important to his future. Another young woman, whose life had been strangely affected by Jimmy, would show him that a strange gift could change his life forever.

Jimmy had died. He was dead; no other word for it. His friends had been at his funeral. Life had changed for him. He had gone from blackness into light and then on to a gray world. What would become of him? Where was he going next, if anywhere? Read on!

Beginnings

"Jimmy, Jimmy! Get yer lazy ass out of that bed or I'll tan yer hide!"

Jimmy sprang out of bed, jumped into his boots, and clambered down the stairs to the kitchen lean-to at the back of the house.

"Where 'ave ya been, ya lazy little sod!" his mother raged at him. "I need the shoppin' done so I kin get yer pa's dinner fer 'im when he gets home from work."

Jimmy waited for his ma to finish her makeup, which consisted of black eyebrow pencil drawn straight across her brows and a lipstick she had bought from Woolies some four years ago and only used on her not too infrequent trips to the Dog and Duck on Inkerbrook Road two streets away from the smelly hovel they called home. The red slash of her mouth looked hideous against her pale, sallow skin, as she opened and closed her mouth to make the lipstick she had drawn across her thin bottom lip smudge onto her top lip with some to spare on her two front teeth, which were about all the teeth she had left.

Jimmy waited, looking disgustedly at his mother. She had a skirt that tightly squashed her flat bottom and was torn up at the side showing far too much of her blue-and-pink-veined, scrawny legs, and a tight blouse that showed her thin chest and fried-egg tits.

Yuck, thought Jimmy, far too smart to have said it aloud and get yet another beating on the head for his trouble.

"Now," she said in her most wheedling voice, "Jimmy, I shall not be long, and I need you to get the food while I am out visiting Maud, me sick friend."

Jimmy sighed. "Yes, Ma," he resigned.

"Now go to the butcher and ask 'im if he has a nice juicy bone for yer dog, then go to Vi's and ask her for as much scrap and bruised vegetables that you can buy fer a farthing, okay?"

Jimmy looked pleadingly at his mother and begged her not to send him to the butcher again. "Ya know the butcher got mad and kicked me out las' time fer lying!" he yelled. "He asked me where me dog was—how was I to know the dog strapped outside his shop belonged to his kids? Ma, he knows we don't 'ave a dog. *Please* don't send me there!"

Jimmy's mother looked at him with contempt. "You 'ad better get me that bone or yer pa will clatter ya as well as me!" she snarled. "Now git out and get the shoppin' now!"

With that, she gave him a smack on the back of his head that he didn't see coming. He ended up sprawled outside the house with half the neighbors laughing and watching the spectacle from their rickety old chairs. Jimmy blushed red to the roots of his hair as his ma thrust the farthing into his hand and went to kick him on his backside. Forgetting her tight skirt, she spun around and landed in the gutter, swearing for all she was worth. The neighbors laughed louder than ever and cat-called her as she struggled to get up in an undignified fashion, showing her underwear and the black elastic that kept her now-torn stockings up. Her left knee was bruised and bleeding. She hobbled back indoors with as much dignity as she could muster, washed her leg with the one tea towel they owned, darned her stockings with huge stitches, slicked a bit of lipstick across her bottom lip, squeezing her lips together, and flounced out of the house.

Jimmy did not hate his ma, although he said he did to his best friends Johnny Green and Don Smale. She was his ma after all. He did, however, hate it when his pa slapped his ma, which often happened when she visited the pub like she was today. He always thought that he ought to be able to defend her, but he had tried once and his pa beat his ears so hard he was deaf for a week and his ma received a bigger beating than usual. So he would try to keep out of the way as soon as his pa knew she was in the pub.

Jimmy saw his friends and got out his brightly colored marbles from his pocket, three scarcies, two ball bearings, which they called balbies, and ten ordinary marbles. The other two boys looked at the scarcies with envy.

"Who wants these two?" he offered with a sly smile on his face.

Don looked at his friend, a huge grin stretching across his face. "I'll 'ave 'em," he shouted with joy, throwing his hand out quickly to grab the very desirable treasure from his friend's hand.

"On yer bike!" shouted Johnny, grabbing Don's hand away and replacing it with his own. "I'll 'ave 'em, Jimmy, me ol' pal!" he smiled. "I can give ya me pa's police whistle that he found yesterday and let me hold on to fer awhile."

Don, not to be outdone, said, "I'll give ya me brother's penknife an' a good suck of me gobstopper."

Jimmy was tempted but then remembered what he wanted. He said, "Right. You want a challenge?"

"Yep," said both boys at once. In both their minds, the scarcies would be soon nestling in their own pockets.

"The challenge is . . ." He looked seriously at both boys in turn. ". . . is the first one that comes back here with a big juicy bone!"

Both lads looked at Jimmy as if he had just dropped out of the sky. They took a few seconds to register that he had been serious before they flew off in two different directions. If Jimmy could have slapped his own back he would have. It was so easy with friends like his. He was excellent at marbles and would soon win them back to his pocket where they belonged. He laughed aloud as he went into Vi's shop, the farthing safely tucked into his sock.

"Hi, Aunty Vi," he said. "Me ma asked me if yer 'ave any bruised vegetables you could let 'er 'ave?"

Vi looked at the scruffy little lad with his skinny legs and scuffed boots at least one size too big for him. Her soft heart went out to him. "Hiya, Jimmy, me little darlin'," she said as she gathered some old potatoes that had been kicking around for a while, a mangy looking turnip, and a few good carrots that she hid under the other vegetables. She held a finger up and tapped the side of her nose. "There ya go, darlin'. That'll be a farthing." She sighed, stretching her back and wincing as the dull pain of overwork and under nourishment caused her shoulders, back, and legs to ache most of the time.

Jimmy was thinking of asking her to let him off the farthing, but when he saw the haggard look on her face, he decided against it. The grocer came out to the front of the store, watching to make sure Vi put the money in the box under the counter.

Vi winked at him as he took his bag up and, smiling,

said a hurried "Ta ta!" He was away from the shop and around the corner before he bit into the bruised apple his aunt had popped into his bag.

Jimmy didn't have to wait long before the lanky frame of his friend Don came into view, with a nice juicy bone clutched tight in his hand.

"Great!" shouted Jimmy.

He was about to snatch the bone from Don's large, skinny fingers when he held it above the shorter boy's head. "Scarcies first, boy, or the deal is off!"

Jimmy reluctantly dug into his pocket and produced the very coveted scarcies. "Here they are then." He dropped them begrudgingly into his friend's outstretched hand.

"Them are beauties," Don said, rattling them together in his hand and then polishing them both on the seat of his well-patched dirty shorts.

Jimmy looked on, regretful of his rashness. He loved those scarcies, but in the back of his mind he was already scheming about how he would get them back.

Johnny came running around the corner with a bone tucked under his arm. He had just stolen it from his dog and it had cost him a nip in his backside, which he rubbed as he held the scruffy, half-chewed bone above his head in triumph. Jimmy and Don laughed at the state of the filthy bone and Don held the scarcies tight in his upstretched hand.

"Oh no!" Johnny wailed. "I got a bite up the ass an' all!"

Don and Jimmy rolled around in laughter as their poor friend grabbed the back of his pants, revealing a nasty bruised backside.

"Where'd you get your bone from anyway?" Don asked between his laughter.

"Stole it from our dog!" he wailed, regretting it now he

didn't even get a sniff of the scarcies. He lifted the bone as if he was going to throw it over Mrs. Tibb's wall when Don stopped him.

"I can take that off your hands for ya," he said craftily.

Johnny was about to sling the stinky bone at his friend when he thought, *Wonder why he wants a smelly old bone.* "Hang on a minute," he said. "What would you want a bone for?"

Don looked a bit sheepish and admitted he had stolen his family's dinner. Both boys laughed out loud at him. "You nitwit!" Jimmy said. "You can't fool yer ma into thinking this dog bone is the one she bought this morning from the butcher!"

Don scowled at him, "Yes, I can. If I wash the thing under the tap in the backyard, she won't know the difference." Both boys rolled with laughter, and then a sudden thought struck Don. "What if I give you some of me balbies?"

Johnny thought about it a minute then, with a huge smile on his face, said, "Seeing it's you, I'll sell it to you for one of those scarcies."

Don was not happy, but he spit on his hand and shook his friend's grubby hand, handing one of the scarcies to him. Jimmy could have cheered, as he knew those scarcies would be back in his pocket where they belonged before tonight.

The boys found an old newspaper on the ground and, using a page to cover the two bones, quickly made a ball out of the rest. With the bones acting as goalposts, they played their own version of football for the next hour.

Jimmy shared his half-eaten apple bite for bite with his two friends then, picking up the right bone, said goodbye to his friends and ran back home. They had arranged to meet later for a game of marbles after each going off for a bit of bread and margarine to keep them going until dinner.

Don sneaked into the backyard that his family shared with four other houses, trying not to trip over the junk that lay scattered knee-deep in places. He made his way to the tap that was shared with the neighbors, as none of the houses had running water. Every house only had gas pipes and new mantles to light the front room and supply gas to stoves, which were second- or third-hand and popped and spluttered and scared them all to death. He turned the tap on, glad that the rush of water took most of the grime off of the half-eaten bone. He swirled it under the tap then put it up to his nose. It didn't smell too bad now that it was cleaner. He sneaked in the back door and was just about to put it back on the scrubbed table when a voice called, "Don! Where you been?"

His mother seemed to appear right behind him; she must have been behind the door as he sneaked in. "What you doing with that bone?" she yelled, snatching it out of his hand. "What on earth have you done to it? Looks as if it's been half eaten." She smacked his ears and threw it onto the table. "How on earth am I going to cook that now?" she shouted, about to hit him again.

"Ma, you don't understand," he sniffled. "I came in earlier and a big black dog grabbed it off of the table, and I had to run like mad and snatch it from him. It fell to the ground and got covered in mud, but I managed to wash it off and get it back for you." He was now blubbering, half convinced by his own story.

"Get out of here," she said, not sure whether to believe his lie or not. She cut a larger slice of bread than usual, spread a little margarine onto it, and handed it over to him. "Eat that then get out of my sight. I suppose once it's in the pan with the potatoes no one will know the difference, but make sure the door is shut tight behind ya in the future, ya hear me?"

Don thought, *Bet the neighbors three streets away can hear her.* Very quietly he replied, "Yes, Ma."

Johnny ran home to the two-bedroom back-to-back houses where his family lived and went into the scruffy kitchen, calling his ma. She came in from the clothesline with clothespins in her mouth and two young children with runny noses and dirty faces clinging to her dress. She took the clothespins out and looked at Johnny, taking in the new tear in the back of his pants and blood smearing his filthy hands.

"What the devil have ya been up to this time, eh?" Before he had time to answer she turned him around and slapped his backside hard. He screeched, as the pain was unbearable. "Don't ya cry or so help me I'll give ya sumpin' to cry for!" she yelled at the eldest and most troublesome of her brood of eight.

She had only been married eight and a half years and had managed to have a baby every year. Her face told the story of everyone in this neighborhood; wrinkled, pinched, and workworn. Her prematurely gray and brown hair hung in a tangled mess that she had neither the time nor the will to do anything with. She would have been depressed if she didn't have so much to do, what with looking after all these babies. Her skinny body was now showing the next baby when she was not yet over the last one.

She looked at her eldest, a little shocked as he cried. More gently, she asked what the trouble was, and reluctantly he pulled his pants down enough to show her the wounds of the dog bite. "How did that happen?" she said. Her voice now held no anger, just a weary tone.

"A big dog bit me," Johnny wailed, taking full advantage of his ma's better side.

She grabbed him to her and stroked his back. "There, there, son. I am sure the dog won't die."

Johnny smiled at his mother's little joke and enjoyed this rare bit of pampering. She smiled at her son, dirt and all; she loved her kids. Cutting him a slice, she went to the cupboard and spread jam instead of margarine on his bread. This was a rare treat, and he hugged his ma before running off to see his friends. The jam was now mixing with the dirt on his tear-streaked, filthy face. He could hear the other kids in his family crying because they were not allowed jam like him. He smiled, feeling warm inside after the attention his ma had given him.

Jimmy got back to his ramshackle home and went straight to the kitchen. His mother was nowhere to be seen. She had left him a thin slice of bread and margarine and scampered off to see her friends down at the pub. Jimmy grabbed the slice after throwing the bone—now covered with a bit of ink from the paper it was wrapped in—on the table along with the vegetables. He stuffed the bread in his mouth all at once, pulled the door closed, and went back out to meet his friends. As he walked, he smiled to himself. He knew he was about to win his best scarcies back.

It was getting dark when he got home, his scarcies feeling warm against his leg as they lay in his pocket where he'd known they would end up. As he opened the door, his ma was waiting in the small hallway. She had changed her clothes and was wearing a really tight dress that showed off her skinny, flat tits and squashed and flattened her bottom. It was far too tight around her slim but bony hips. It had been an expensive dress when it was new, but had had at least ten owners before her. She had seen it at the market and, although it was far too small for her, bought it along with two pairs of underwear that were not too white (she thought a bit of a boil would fix that) and an old flannel nightie for the princely sum of a penny.

She remembered the weight of her hubby's fist that night with a flinch. He had insisted on her taking her purchases right back, but she offered him what he couldn't refuse so he eventually gave in and had his way with her twice that night.

She glared at the look of disgust on her son's face and in her wheedling voice said, "When yer pa gets back tell I'm I've gone to Nancy's. He won't mind."

Jimmy was at once scared. "Oh, Ma, don't make me lie fer ya again. Pa threatened to kill me the last time."

His ma gave him one of her gap-toothed smiles and kissed the top of his head. "Be a good boy fer yer ma," she coaxed.

Jimmy, unsure what to say, was between a rock and a hard place. If he didn't agree to lie to his pa, she would smack his ears and still go out, knowing that he wouldn't tell on her anyway. If he told his pa the truth, he would hit him for not stopping her and hit her as soon as she got back or, worst of all, go down to the Dog and Duck and drag her home by her hair and pummel both of them again. What was he to do? He could feel tears prickling the back of his eyes and sniffed to hold them back.

"Ahh, is he going to miss his ma then?" she said in her mocking voice.

At that moment he hated her with all the passion of an

eight-year-old. "Ma, I am worried about you. Ya know what Pa's like. One of these days he might kill you, and what will happen to me!"

"Shut yer mouth!" she shouted at him. "You always was a crybaby." Then as soon as she realized that he looked really hurt, she changed back into the cringing voice that coaxed her way in or out of anything with her only child. "Ah, me duck, I am sorry but I need to have me fun, same as you playing out with yer friends. S'no different, is it.?"

Jimmy knew he was beaten. "Please be back to cook Pa's dinner, Ma," he pleaded, a lost look on his eight-year-old face.

"Yeah, I'll only be a half hour. Promise," she said, triumph in her voice as she grabbed her coat and was out of the door singing "Goodbye, duck!" as she hurried away toward the pub and her bit of fun.

Jimmy poked at the fire to get a little heat from it and decided he would put some more coal from the bucket on it. If he had to be here waiting for his ma to get back he would just as well be warm. It was getting quite dark, and Jimmy knew where a few candles were kept in a box under the stairs. Better still, he knew where the paraffin lamp that his pa had bought from the market was. He had shown him how to light it and pump it up to get the best light and how to fill it from the can they had under the stairs.

Gingerly, he shook the lamp to see if there was any paraffin left in it as he had seen his pa do. Yes! It was about half full. He reached up to the mantle and grabbed the matches. Following carefully what his pa had shown him to do, he soon had the lamp glowing if spitting a bit from the cheap paraffin his pa had gotten from his work. When he had asked where his pa got the paraffin from, he remembered he had tapped his nose the way grown-ups did when they were telling you a secret or telling you to mind your own.

Jimmy was really pleased with himself as he sat in his pa's chair with his feet up near the fireplace. His short legs couldn't reach the mantle like his pa's could but at least he could pretend for a while he was in charge.

"Pa," he snarled, "get me a cup of tea an' put sugar in this time, ya lazy cow! Ma, get me food now—I'm starving! Pa, clean out the coalhouse, ya lazy bugger! I need it spotless by the time I get in from work!"

He was having so much fun he didn't hear the door open until his pa's face pushed right up close to his. He snarled, "Oh yeah, ya would love to order yer ma and me around, but I got news fer ya: It ain't gonna happen! Now git yer ass out of my chair, ya bugger, and make me a brew before I hit ya!"

Jimmy jumped up, grabbing the kettle from the stove and leaving to fill it at the outside tap. When he got back with the steaming cup, his pa was stretched out with his mouth open, snoring. The smell of beer filled the room, his holey boots were thrown down on the fender, and his big fists were not bunched but relaxed in sleep. Jimmy quickly placed the tea down on the fender, having heaped sugar into it the way his pa liked it. Frightened to wake him and now worried about his ma, he crept silently out of the house.

He stumbled his way down Inkerbrook Road to the Dog and Duck, peering in through the door to the smoke-filled, yeasty smelling room till his eyes focused. There was Ma's haggard face, her toothy grin and eyes toward a greasy looking character who openly had his hand halfway up her skinny thigh. His other hand held a pint of stout, a cigarette hung from the corner of his mouth, and the sick look of a drunken perve lined his greasy face.

Jimmy felt sick to his stomach. If his pa could see this going on he would murder the pair of them! He stared across the pub, whispering loudly, "Ma, Ma!" She turned her face toward him and ignored him. "Ma, Ma!" he persisted. She turned her back as if she wanted nothing to do with him.

He tried once more when the barman caught his eye. "Git outta here! Yer not old enough," he joked, but he gave a stern look toward Jimmy as his eyes flicked toward the outside. Jimmy knew he had to get his ma out of there before his pa woke up hungry and mad.

He ran around to the side of the pub and saw a window just out of his reach. He looked around and found an old crate and a wooden vegetable box. They were both a bit battered, but Jimmy stood them one on top of the other and, climbing unsteadily up, he was able to stare in the window. His ma was closer still to the greasy looking bloke, her head tilted back and her skirt even higher. He couldn't make out where the creep's hands were, but he had seen enough.

He tapped on the window and a few heads turned in his direction, but not his ma's. He tapped a bit louder and shouted, "Ma, Ma!" She turned to the direction of the window and quickly waved him away with a thunderous look. Jimmy was scared now. He knew he had to tell her about Pa.

He tapped none too softly this time and shouted, "Ma, yer gonna get it! Me pa's back, and if he knew ya were here with 'im, he'd kill ya! Ma, Ma!"

The crowd at the bar began laughing, fit to bust, but the barman was very unhappy. "Ya better go see what he wants, Flo, or he'll keep me customers from their drinks." The boozy customers were too busy laughing to take much notice of the warning in the barman's tone.

Flo reluctantly detangled herself from her rough and randy partner and, fuming, marched to the door. Jimmy, seeing her move, reached over too far and fell head over ass off of the now-broken boxes, scraping his knees and banging his head. He howled in pain and heard the customers inside howling louder with drunken laughter. A few of them stepped outside, pints still in their hands, to watch the antics.

Jimmy hobbled toward his ma who smacked his ears in her fury at him. "Oh, Ma!" he yelled, "I'm already hurting."

"You'll get more if ya ain't got a bloody good reason fer getting me outta there." She pointed back over her shoulder.

"Me pa's home, and he is asleep fer a minute, but if he wakes and there's no tea he'll most likely kill me and you. Come home now *please*, Ma!"

She looked a bit less angry now, but in her booze-filled madness she was not going anywhere. "Look, Jimmy," she slithered. "I'll be 'alf an hour, promise. He'll more 'an likely sleep fer another couple of hours anyway."

Jimmy looked at her, frightened at how this was all going to come crashing down on his and his ma's ears. He knew there was nothing he could do but walk away and go back home. How he hated his ma at that moment. She was a greedy, self-satisfying bitch, and he hated her. He kicked a stone so hard it went right over someone's wall, and he ran as fast as his legs could carry him away from the tinkling of broken glass.

When he got into the house, his pa was still asleep, snoring so loudly the neighbors were thumping on the wall. He crept in and waited in terror should he wake this sprawled man who was his pa.

Time ticked slowly by. *It must be half an hour now,* he thought. There was no sign of his ma. He didn't know what to do. If his pa woke up and there was no dinner, he would go berserk. Time went on. Another half hour, then another, and still no sign of his ma! Inside he was quaking with terror. What was keeping the selfish cow? Eventually he knew that she was not coming back for quite some time, and he thought he had better start the stew. He had seen his ma do it a few times. He would be all right, he told himself.

In the kitchen the stove with a wonky leg seemed to grin at him. *What, you cook?* It seemed to mock him. Jimmy got the big frying pan his ma used to brown the bone in. He opened the oven and spooned dripping into the pan and lit the spattering gas ring. He unwrapped the bone and dropped it into the hot fat. It sizzled and spat hot dripping all over the stove and at him. He turned his back and cut the vegetables in chunks as he had seen his ma do. The meat smelled lovely. When the smell filled the kitchen, he remembered to turn the piece over. It sizzled and spat again. Now what did his ma do next? He thought for awhile. Well, somehow the vegetables had to be cooked and it was something to do with water. His young mind tried to conjure up how his ma cooked them.

Suddenly, the meat didn't smell so nice and bluish smoke started to rise from the pan. Jimmy lifted the vegetables up and dropped them into the smoky pan. Flames burst into the air as the damp vegetables hit the pan. Jimmy, terrified, threw the contents of the kettle straight into the pan. Whoosh! The flames leapt to the ceiling, filling the room with dense smoke that was at once choking Jimmy. He struggled out of the kitchen, flames leaping though behind him. He hurried toward his sleeping pa, pulling at his arm.

"Pa! Pa!" he shouted, coughing and spluttering.

His pa's lungs were already half filled with the smoke, and he was more dead than alive as he continued to take in large, snoring lungs full of the deadly smoke. Jimmy's head started to pound as he tried desperately to awaken his pa. Tears of frustration then a choking cough pulled him down to the floor. He saw the staggering form of his mother being struck by falling concrete as he sunk into oblivion.

How shocked his friends had been when they, with scrubbed faces, watched his little coffin being dropped on top of his ma and pa's bigger black coffins in the pauper's area of the churchyard. The ceremony was soon over as the dirt was shoveled quickly back in the hole and the gravedigger rushed over to the third funeral that morning.

Jimmy sat on top of the mound and looked at his friends' faces. Tears streaked their stricken faces. The scarcies they had found in the ashes of his home didn't seem so much of a find when they stared at the mound, not seeing Jimmy there smiling as always and trying desperately to cheer them up. He looked up and whoosh! He was half pulled, half eager to go into the tunnel of light that led on and on, getting more bright than he had ever seen in all of his life. Colors were sweeping around him like a vast circular rainbow as up and forward he traveled. He awoke in a beautiful blue room with people whispering in hushed voices that they were not too sure what to do with him. His parents were over as well, and as he drifted back into a deep sleep he was slightly aware that he was being taken to his parents, wherever they were . . .

Jimmy took the piece of wood he was trying to float on the water. It was his imaginary boat out of here. He looked wistfully at it. He had hollowed out the center as best he could and had attached an old scruffy piece of cloth that his mother had been using as a duster.

She had long ago given up on the idea of dusting, as the air was so full of dust and dirt that whenever the wind blew, it unceasingly brought it all right back into their squalid little shack. She soon realized that the task was useless, as was washing anything or trying to get themselves clean or dry. This place was the most disgusting she had ever known, and boy had she lived in some slums in her time. Bedwater Road had been the worst. It was a two-story mid-terrace property, where rats ran in and out of each house and lice crawled up the walls, but nothing had prepared her for this evil smelling, rank place. She hated everything about it—including her worthless husband and miserable brat of a son. She was happy for him to be out all day and night, although there didn't seem to be a difference in this foul place. The nights were only slightly darker than the days.

Jimmy plunged the homemade boat into the foul, murky water, and immediately it subsided the rag, now drenched in the filthy, scummy water. Jimmy swore loudly and lasciviously and picked up the boat, crashing it down with all of his force in his frustration. "Nuffin' ever works here! I hate it here!"

He heard his mother shouting, "Get here, ya little sod!"

What fer, another beating? he thought to himself. *Not*

lightly! He stormed out of the water and across the sharp stones that bruised his bare feet while the thorns tore the flesh of his legs and arms. He tried to get as far away as possible from the awful, screechy voice of his inadequate mother. At last he could not hear her nagging anymore, so he settled down quietly to watch out for anyone who was walking around. He climbed a tree and settled as carefully as he could to spend the night away from his wretched parents and the slum that was now his only place of refuge.

He soon fell asleep, his skinny arms wrapped around his tired, sore, thin legs, the mournful sound of the place helping him to drift off instead of scaring him like it once had. He enjoyed his dreams when he got the chance to sleep, which was usually broken by the seemingly endless racket of his parents fighting. His name was always mentioned for having committed some misdemeanor or another! But for now he slept and dreamt.

From Light to Dark

Across the vastness of space the light ones traveled, growing in brilliance with each passing day. The missions in the Shadow Lands were slow and continuous; however, the rewards were great to these loving, generous souls. Each selfless deed meant a lighter existence with new and more beautiful planes of existence to discover and rest in.

Light ones were steadfast and exacting in their teachings and would use only the best and most loving for any of the duties they had in mind. That is why they choose very carefully the two young women whom best suited this extra special task.

Many workers were involved in some way or another to assist the light ones in their tasks, receiving as their own rewards status and power in their own small groups. They would also gravitate endlessly to a brighter level of existence, to eventually become light ones themselves.

Amongst the more exulted groups was a band of wholly dedicated new workers. These workers had not long ago come over from the Shadow Lands, rescued and accepted by the brothers and sisters of the movement. These clansmen were working their way through their own karmas and were glad of any new blood. Each worker was lovingly taught and guided by the light ones and put into groups that could best use their special qualities. The groups that took the very best of the quality workers were named the House of Destiny, Harmony, Gentleness, Humbleness, and Beauty. Amongst these groups were two young females who had been taught diligently and with great love and care that patience and dedication were needed for a very special assignment, an assignment that would earn them the title of light one. How proud the whole group was to know that these very special girls were from their groups. There was no such thing as selfishness amongst the evolved ones, only pride as a whole group. Had anyone of them shown any sign of a negative trait they would not have been able to join them. The chosen girls were delighted and proud to have been selected and chattered and laughed with their delighted friends.

Melody was small in stature with large, soulful green eyes that were full of sadness one moment and twinkled in delight the next. She was kind and patient and loving. Melody had been delighted to know she'd been accepted into the House of Gentleness and was to go on a very special mission. Her heart and chest swelled with love and pride.

Dorinda, the other young woman, had spent several more years in the darkness of the Shadow Lands. It had seemed like an eternity to this girl who was unable to forgive herself for the crime she had committed against humanity. Weary and wretched, she had arrived into the lighter skies to be lovingly cared for and nurtured by the other workers and light ones that were sent to help her. Dorinda watched Melody from the sideline and saw a beautiful young woman who seemed to glow as she smiled. She so wanted to show the light ones that the trust that they had put onto the shoulders of Melody and her was justified and that she and Melody were willing and able to complete the task that had been set for them.

The light ones that had taught both Melody and Dorinda were delighted by their progress and smiled benignly at their prized pupils. They wished them well and faded back into the distance, leaving the girls to get on with their task. They hugged each other and began walking swiftly down the road that would eventually lead them to the Shadow Land. Both young women shivered in delight and dread, for they were to reach into the evil Shadow Lands and bring home the child.

The dark ones that lived in the Shadow Lands lead a very difficult different existence, with scant shelter, squalor, darkness, and meager possessions. The further into the Shadow Lands one ventured, the darker and more miserable they became. Forests of a most dismal type covered most of the land, and no leaves or blossoms adorned the boughs. The fruit, if any, were gray and shriveled like the misshapen trees that existed there. Nothing of beauty existed there. Swamplands or dry sharp stones plagued the dark ones, and filth covered their garments and skin. There were no seasons, no sun, moon, or stars to gaze up at, just the irritating wind that blew the repulsive smells of the swampland into every area. The evil smell cloyed their nostrils and invaded their bodies and hair.

The dark ones were unpleasant to each other and despised the workers that came from time to time to help them, or at least to give them some respite. The dark ones, never realizing that the light ones were perhaps their only hope. They saw them as interfering and loathsome, just there to mock them. It was not that they didn't know, but the cold, dark, unforgiving land they dwelled in had warped their minds and corrupted what little was left of their dignity and wholesomeness. They didn't realize that they didn't need to stay in this godforsaken land, so they used every opportunity to be obnoxious and cruel to the helpers, their only real hope and sanity in this insane, grotesque land. They threw filth at them and were incensed when the filth refused to soil the helpers' clothes. It just rolled back and covered the dark ones again with more rotten smelling filth than before. They howled their anger and tried to attack the workers. Usually the workers caught on very quickly and faded back into obscurity, for they knew that in this odious place they were not completely safe, so they had to rely on their cloaks of security that made them fade and blend in with the background.

The dark ones tried to live in some sort of community but failed miserably, as their jealousy, greed, and tortured minds meant that a lot of them stole from each other or abused each other at every opportunity. For every evil deed they committed, they were forced back into even darker planes with whatever they had stolen or lost. So they existed in very small groups of two to three. Every now and then one might come across hate-filled husbands and wives, sworn enemies, or victims unable to forgive the perpetrator that had caused an atrocity in their life and the perpetrator of this crime forced to live as if melded to each other until the passion of hate had passed on.

In the case of a lot of the dark ones, they preferred to be alone in their own hell, where they hid from others. Uncivilized, filthy, deformed by atrocities they had inflicted onto others and themselves, they lived miserably in this solitary, dismal way. Alone, they could hide their ugliness and deformities in the darkness that surrounded them. These tortured dark ones could sometimes be heard lamenting, crying out in piteous self-loathing, disgusted, unable to help themselves, and unwilling or unable to be helped by others. Only when they began to feel the need for contact and love would their existence start to lighten.

Melody's Story

As the helpers started down the road toward the dark planes, they chatted, the sun warm and their spirits high, as their laughter and lighthearted banter gave way to more serious topics. Melody spoke quietly, a new sadness etched on her beautiful face.

"Dorinda, may I tell you something?" she asked in a small voice full of despair.

Dorinda smiled down at the lovely face and reached for her hand. "Anything," she whispered back, thinking how much Melody looked like a frightened doe, her eyes wide and glazed as if caught in a trap.

Melody began, "My husband Edward and I lived an idyllic life in the countryside. He was a gentleman farmer, and we loved the life. He had three sisters that occasionally stayed with us, and life was happy then with their laughter and chatter. They filled the house with joy and freshness. Every day they were there was a special one for me; I had missed the vitality and chatter of younger women. That was tragically all to change when Maud, the eldest sister, a pretty girl so full of life, happy-go-lucky, and loving, died of scarlet fever when she had just turned nineteen. We were all heartbroken and things were never the same again. Mary,

24

the second sister, was only seventeen at this time and so bright and vivacious. She ended up married to a lawyer and gave birth to seven children, six girls and a boy. The daughters were such sweet little things and Oliver, the youngest, was a real cherub. I truly think they would have carried on having babies if Olly had not arrived."

Melody sighed, and her friend slipped her hand into hers again and smiled gently at her. Melody continued, "That only leaves Violet, the baby sister of Edward's. She was fifteen when her sister died, a wistful child but with a bubbly sense of fun. She never married; I think she was put off by seeing her sister bulging with babies nearly every year."

Dorinda laughed, "I can see why!"

Melody laughed with her and continued, glad for the strength she was given by Dorinda. "I was an only child and my parents were quite strict, believing children should be seen and not heard. They loved me but I think as soon as I was married they breathed a sigh of relief."

Both young women laughed, and Melody continued.

"Edward and I had a lovely, big, white-and-blue cottage with large windows and a view out of every one of them. To the front we looked over a vast expanse of trees and green grass. The trees were of every kind and color that blended together in several different shades of fresh greens, browns, mulberry, and wine, with blossoms of pink, white, and yellow in the spring and summer. Occasionally wild pheasants, with their magnificent plumage, flew by. I used to worry about them during the shooting season, but Edward only used to laugh at me and call me silly."

Melody looked down, but soon was in free flow again.

"To the back of the house we could see more splendid trees, the village green, and field upon field like a patchwork quilt. Sometimes the bleating of lambs or the low, mournful lowing of cattle was heard as the farmers went about their farms. Edward and I, as I said before, had an idyllic life, apart from one thing we needed: children to fill this cottage with their noise and clatter. After ten years of marriage and having tried every doctor or specialist, no luck. It would all end the same. "Sorry, Mr. and Mrs. Blake, but we have tried everything and although your body is young and strong, for some unknown reason you cannot conceive a child. Go and enjoy your life; perhaps later you might consider adoption or fostering a child." Somehow this did not appeal to us. We wanted our own sons to inherit Edward's livelihood when he grew too old and weak and at least one daughter to spoil.

"Month after month, the same result. Then one spring day when I was thirty, I started to feel unwell. This was something I was not used to, as my health was generally excellent. I was ill in the mornings and felt irritable and scratchy, and now and again I would be mean to Edward when he asked me how I was feeling. I would storm at him, 'How do I look?'

"We decided that I had better see the family physician, as even after three weeks I was still unwell and getting weak. Dr. Thatcher listened to all I had to say and then asked me how my bosom felt. I could see in his eye that Edward was bristling.

"'Well, to tell you the truth,' I said, "my bosom was sore and heavy."

"'Hmm,' said the doctor, "You, my good woman, are not ill. You are going to be a mother.'"

"'A mother!' I said, my eyes filled with tears of joy. "I am going to have—to have a baby!"

"Well," said the doctor in delight, "do you feel as though you need a tonic?"

"Edward and I looked at each other's beaming faces. 'No, I think this news is tonic enough.'

"Dr. Thatcher patted Edward on the shoulder, shook his hand, and embraced me. 'Deary me,' he sighed. 'If only I could give all of my patients the same good news. Excluding Miss Phipps, my next patient—she is sixty-three and a born spinster.' We all laughed as we left the office on a high note.

"Edward cared for me as if I was a prize specimen. He fussed and coddled me each and every day throughout the pregnancy, and when it was time for me to be confined go on bed rest he got the best midwife that money could buy and waited impatiently, walking up and down the corridor.

"I did not expect the extreme pains that went on and on, and hour after hour the pain grew stronger and stronger until I though that I was going to die. The midwife, a plain looking woman with a hairy mole on the end of her nose and a grim look on her face (that meant she was taking no prisoners), thrust a bone between my teeth. 'Right, my girl, bite down on this and push through your behind.' I did as I was told, too scared of what other little treats might be in her black bag. I pushed and she waited. I pushed and pushed, then in anger the midwife screeched, 'Come on!' She yelled at me, slapping me firmly on the thigh. 'You are not trying! Now, bite down and this time when the pain comes push as if your life depended on it. Your little one's life does!' Hearing this, I found the strength from somewhere and screamed as I felt as if I was terribly constipated. 'Good!' she yelled. 'Now keep it coming, I can see your baby's head.'

"I pushed with all the strength I could muster and still needed to push again. Then, just faintly, I felt a slithering and wetness between my legs and the midwife beamed at me. 'It's a daughter! You have a girl!' This tiny scrap that I could feel wriggling between my thighs was my daughter! Soon there was the sound of slapping and the oh-so-joyful sound of my baby's first cry. It was loud and lusty. I cried tears of joy. The midwife's face was a little concerned as she washed the baby and placed her into my arms. 'She is a little bit blue,' she said then she shook her head. 'No, I am sure she is fine. Some babies are a little blue but it will go in a day or two.'

"So our beautiful little girl was born. We named her Louise and right away she could twist us around her miniature little finger. We loved her so much. Edward burst into the nursery as soon as I was presentable and looked lovingly at our precious baby girl and me. 'You did well, my dear,' he said, tears glistening in his eyes. 'Maybe next time you can produce a boy to keep her safe,' he said, a beaming smile pulling the sides of his mouth. I remember I was sore and tired, but I felt the love of my husband flowing around me. I glowed with pride and love for them both, my new and precious family."

Dorinda sighed. "I have never known the pleasure of being a mother.".

Her friend, smiling, said, "My dear, there is no feeling quite like it. Louise grew steadily day by day, and at two she was walking, chattering, and getting into everything. We would laugh at the way she said 'No' to everything we asked her and then got annoyed with herself when she realized she had said no to a treat. She was so beautiful with huge blue eyes like her papa and my strawberry blonde hair. She never did lose that slight blueness around her mouth, but the doctor had said she was fine, so we were now ignoring it as an unimportant part of our dear little girl.

"When she was three she would want to run everywhere, her little legs pumping as she ran. Then gradually she started to get breathless after a little run, so we took her back to the doctors. He was a bit concerned and advised that we take her to the specialist in London. We were very anxious about her now, and I found that I had to watch her constantly. I was getting so tired myself that Edward insisted I go to bed early that night and sleep in our room. He said she would be fine with the nurse we employed to look after her. As we were to travel to London the next day, this did make sense.

"I slept as I hadn't done for months. The nurse came crashing into our bedroom before daybreak, in a state of panic. 'The little lamb,' she kept saying as Edward flew out of the bedroom and sped off toward the east wing where the nurse and our beloved baby slept.

"I heard a shout of, 'No! My God, noooo!' followed by a huge cry. I rushed past the gibbering nurse and down to the nursery where my beloved husband sat and nursed our very blue daughter.

"'What has happened? Is she okay?' I asked, my heart thudding deafeningly in my chest and my eyes not believing what I was seeing.

"He turned to me heartbrokenly and cried. 'Our beautiful Louise has gone, my darling. Our baby is dead.' I could and would not believe it. 'Nooo!' I kept repeating. 'She can't have! Do something!'

"It was no good. She was gone. I could not accept it, and I knew that had I been there when she needed me she would be still here. I fretted and mourned my dear little girl and no one, not even my dear husband or Dr. Thatcher, could help me. I was in a very dark place, and eventually I could not even eat, drink, or live."

Dorinda hugged her friend. "And now?" she asked.

"Well, now that I have spent a long time with regret and unhappiness I realize that no one could have saved my beautiful Louise. She had a generic disorder of the heart and lungs, and even if she had got past three years old, it would have meant she would not have lived much beyond seven and then spent the majority of that time in pain. I did not want that for her. When I realized that my own slow recovery was affecting so many people, I realized that I must see the truth and move on."

The girls moved forward on their journey and knew that before they reached the boundary of the Shadow Lands they would need to rest and conserve their strength for tomorrow. They came to a small hamlet where the light ones had arranged beds for them and knocked on the door. The girls chose to sleep in a twin room rather than spending the night alone in a strange place. They soon settled in for the night warm, cozy, and safe.

Dorinda's Story

Both girls slept quite well for the first part of the night and probably would have completed the night that way had Dorinda not woken with a start. She heard the screech of an owl flying overhead and woke Melody by sitting up and shouting. Melody was out of bed in an instant and began comforting Dorinda, who was a bit shaken.

"It's all right, Dorinda, I am here. It was only a stupid owl."

Dorinda soon settled back again but could not sleep. She whispered to her friend asking if she was still awake and when Melody said yes, Dorinda said, "If you are not too tired I would like to tell you about my life."

"I would enjoy that," said Melody. "Should I turn on the light?"

"No, please don't. It will make it a lot easier for me to be honest if you can't see my face."

The older girl protested, "I am sure your story can be no worse than mine!"

"Believe me, my dear friend, it is." She sighed deeply and continued. "My name is not really Dorinda, but who in the professional world would be impressed with Jane Smith? Let me start at the beginning," she sighed. "My family was not well off. Pa did what he could, but he and Ma produced a child for nearly every year that they were married and times were extremely hard. I am not telling you this for sympathy because what I was a party to was absolutely terrifying and despicable, and the last thing I deserve is sympathy.

"I was the eldest of twelve children who were all loved by Ma and Pa. Though with Pa you could see the resentment on his face when we needed clothes, extra food, or anything at all. It meant that he would have to spend less time in the Three Ferrets Pub with his pals. He used to say to Ma that if he worked for his money he should at least be able to spend it how he liked. Ma very often got a swollen jaw when she spent too much on food or clothes for us all."

Melody looked shocked, as she had never heard the like. She had such an easy life and, although her parents had been relieved when she married, they or anyone else she knew had never suffered violence of this sort. No one had ever raised a hand to her, and her parents, although they had a cool relationship, had never been violent to each other. They had a cool indifference toward each other and her at times, but she knew they loved each other and her in their own way.

Dorinda continued, "When Ma realized that she had yet another baby on the way, she whispered to me that I had better get a job. I was quite proud and happy to do so, and the money I earned would help Ma support our new baby brother or sister. After a bit of organizing, I was to work for Mr. and Mrs. Barton-Jones who owned a huge mansion with lush gardens and a tennis court. They had two children who each owned their own ponies and went trotting off all dressed up, the girl riding side-saddle in her beautiful gowns and the boy with a hat and jacket like the grown-ups. Little dears, they seemed, on their ponies, but they were horrid to us staff and called us 'riffraffs' and told lies about us to their father who would reprimand even though he knew we had not done anything. He would give us a half smile and a little cough and say, 'How would it look if I took your word against my own children? No, that would never do.' Then he'd disappear upstairs again. The cook, who was in charge of the kitchen staff and under-stair maids, would bite her tongue and say nothing until she and the butler, her husband, got together later.

"We slept in the attic, three of us to a bed, which we were all used to, as we all came from large families. The cook and butler slept next door and, as the walls seemed to be paper-thin, we could hear all that they were saying. Very often we did our best to ignore them, but when the cook was getting annoyed her voice raised up a bit. She was ranting to her husband about the children, but he refused to see any wrong in them. He had his reputation to keep up as head of downstairs and was often spoken to by the lady and gentleman of the house, so even if he did agree with his wife he would never take her side. This was then passed down to the scullery maids and the under-stair maids and every other person that worked under the cook. The day after she had had 'words' with her husband, she would be snippy and unkind to all of us. We just skirted around her and avoided getting in her way for fear of retribution.

"My day would begin at 5:30 and last until bedtime at 9:00. I was allowed one half day off a week or one whole day a month if I forfeited the half days. I would take the full day and go home to help my ma with the children and give her my complete wages, as she needed every last farthing I could give her. I was pleased to give this to her, as we were given two day dresses and a smart dress for special occasions and we had plenty of the cook's marrow bone soup and porridge. When they had a party upstairs, often we would get the leftovers. We were well catered for. I loved my ma and pa and all of my brothers and sisters, so it was no sacrifice."

Dorinda sighed, "I wish I could have stayed that way forever, but life was about to change for me in a way I would not have thought possible. One spring day I was singing to myself as I cleaned out the fire so I could light it later that day in the guest room. I never realized that someone was listening to me, as we were told to just go in with our heads bowed, clean and lay the fires, and then go on to the next fire without looking around. Well, I was shocked when this male voice said to me, 'Why, that is a pretty voice you have, young lady.' I was in awe, as I had never seen a guest before and had never been able to speak with anyone. The lady of the house was kind but insisted that we learn our place very quickly and would punish anyone who tried to step up above their place, as she put it.

"I said, 'Oh, I am so sorry. I didn't know there was anyone staying in this room.' I tried to rush out the door, my job only half completed.

"'Wow,' he laughed. 'I am not going to eat you.' I explained that I was not allowed to speak to guests, as I would be punished. He smiled at me and said, 'Listen, what if the lady of the house came in here and found out you had not completed your job? I think you would be in a lot more trouble. If you don't tell anyone I spoke to you and just go on with your work and sing as you did just now, we will not tell anyone and you will not be in trouble.' I felt very worried, but he gave me a reassuring smile and sat back down in his chair, looking outside at the gardens, bordered by forests and grasslands. I was shocked but afraid not to comply with his wishes so I bent down again.

"The next day I crept into his room, thinking he might have forgotten and been asleep. I began scooping ashes and singing very self-consciously and almost in a whisper. The guest quietly listened and we said no more. As I was about to leave he turned to me and said, 'I will keep your little secret, and as I am here for two weeks I shall expect you to sing for me every morning.' I protested that I was breaking all of the rules by even being in the same room as a guest. He smirked and said, 'Too late for that one, missy. You have broken too many rules already.'

"I was shocked and knew that I should have gone right then and there to the cook and taken my punishment, but I was so afraid that she might dismiss me and send me home in disgrace that I said I would sing for him again the next morning. The guest, who was a very dashing looking man, smiled at me and said, 'Good. We can now be partners in crime.'

"I did not know what to do and was fidgety all day, thinking the owners may have been testing me to see if I was a good girl or not. I cried myself to sleep that night knowing that I had to break the rules the next day and every day while this man was a guest at the house. I could have just closed the door quietly and gone about my cleaning elsewhere.

"As soon as I entered the room the next day, the guest put his hand out as if to touch me and I jumped back. I would have left right away had he not dropped his hand and opened the door wider for me. I had no choice but to go in as he closed the door softly behind us. I really did not feel good about this and thought I should rush the job and get out of there as soon as possible. I busied myself and suddenly felt a tap on my shoulder.

"'Come on, missy, a deal is a deal. Stop rushing and sing for me.' I froze for a second but knew I had to go through with this. I sang and he listened in his chair at the other side of the room. I knew he did not look out the window this time, as I could feel his eyes burning into my back. I had finished the fire and was just about to leave as the guest came across the room in two strides. 'Don't be afraid; I am not going to attack you. If I had wanted that, I would have taken it on the first day I saw you,' he drawled. I blushed hotly and took a quick step back. 'I love to hear you singing and that is all, so please don't look so scared,' he tried to reassure me.

"'Here,' he said, pressing some chocolate into my hand. I had never had chocolate in my whole life and though very tempted, I refused. 'Look, I will keep it in my room,' he said, 'if you are afraid the cook might get suspicious.' I must have looked like a scared rabbit as I refused again and swept out of the door. I could hear his chuckle as I hurried across the hallway to the back stairs and cook's eagle eye.

"'I hope you're not up to no good,' she snarled, 'or you will be out on your ear, my girl.' I lied to assure the cook that I was a good girl and was just feeling a bit out of sorts. She believed me and got the scullery maid to make me a cup of tea and put some sugar in it, a rare luxury. I sipped my tea and almost blurted out my story, but the image of my ma, pa, and the children's disgraced faces stopped me in time. The cook would never believe that I only sang to the guest, and even if she did, I was in for it if she ever found out.

"By the second week I was enjoying my little bits of chocolate and was getting quite used to singing to the handsome guest. I would forget my place sometimes and chat with him. He told me he was very rich and owned lots of gentlemen's clubs and employed several girls to entertain his gentlemen guests. He winked at me. 'If you agree, then there could be a job for you with four times what you earn here plus your own bedroom and maid,' he said. I was flabbergasted and never in a million years would have thought that I could be so lucky."

Dorinda swallowed hard with a lump in her throat, but she continued.

"Daniel Blackman was the guest's name, and he said he would clear it with the lord and lady of the house. And if I was willing, we would leave together in his coach at the end of the week. If I was willing! I was more than willing—I was over the moon! I was told not to mention it to anyone and that he would make all the arrangements. I was so happy I could not keep from smiling and singing as I went about my duties. The cook seemed happy, as she and the others liked to hear me sing.

"The day before we were due to leave, Daniel asked me to come up to his room to go over the plans he had for me. Oh, Melody, I was so young and naïve. I really did believe he wanted to talk to me. I was to tell no one. As soon as I knew the others were asleep, I pulled on my old robe over my nightdress and quietly went to his room. He was dressed up quite smartly in a smoking jacket and had the room lit with candles with a bottle of wine and two glasses on the table. I told him that if he had another guest I could catch up with him early the next day. 'No, missy,' he said, 'this is our wine. We need to celebrate your future.' I could see no wrong in it, Melody, no wrong."

Melody hushed Dorinda and asked her to continue.

"Well, I was flattered and a bit excited so I thought,

Why not? I drank two full glasses and soon realized that I should not have as my head started to spin a bit. Daniel said I would be all right and that another glass would help. I thought he was being kind and gulped down another glass full of the sweet-tasting wine. After that it was all a blur. I remember Daniel lifting me up and saying I needed to lie on his bed for a while, and then he undressed me, reassuring me that all was well. He slipped the covers over me, and a little later as I was drifting in and out of sleep he got in beside me and held me close. It felt good to have a strong man's arms around me. Then he was touching me in a strange sort of way and I began to enjoy it, as it felt so right in my drunken stupor. I felt him get on top of me and then fire between my legs. At that moment, I realized that this man had duped me; we were not here to talk at all. He wanted my body, and my body, although I tried hard to control it, wanted this to happen.

"I must have dropped off to sleep, as the next thing I knew I was being pulled out of bed by my hair and slapped quite hard across the face. 'Why, you dirty little trollop!" the cook snapped as she hit me three or four times on my head and back. She had found me in the guest room, and before I knew it, I was paraded before the mistress where I was told to give back all of my clothes and dismissed without a penny. My dresses had to be handed back, and they would later tell my parents why I had been thrown out in disgrace.

"I put on the only dress that I had, which was the one I came to work there in. I had no money and my reputation was in tatters because I broke the rules. I sobbed as I was literally thrown out the backdoor with all the staff glaring at me. I sobbed my way along the road and realized that I could not go back to my family in disgrace and walked in the opposite direction. I had walked about a mile feeling hurt, dirty, disgusted with myself, and so lonely.

"I saw a coach following me, and it stopped up ahead. I turned my face away as I passed it, afraid that anyone on board would see what a disgrace I was. Just as I passed by, a familiar voice called after me. 'Hi, missy, do you need a lift?' I looked up into the smiling eyes of Daniel Blackman.

"I tore my eyes away from his face and cried, 'Haven't you done enough to me already? Humiliation is taking its toll on me! Offering me a lift is taking it a bit too far, even for a cad like you!'

"I ran as fast as I could, and my eyes were so full of tears that I missed my step and went down hard. A fire of pain consumed my ankle and I just sat there sobbing, wishing that it had been my neck. I laid back on the grass, unable anymore to cope with this pain and self-disgust. How could I have given away my maidenhood so freely? And to a man who had hoodwinked me into believing that he could offer me a fantastic job singing in one of his clubs, the thing I had always wanted to do! I just cried my eyes out and wished only for death.

"I must have passed out with pain and exhaustion, for the next thing I was aware of was someone lifting me like a child and holding me close so that I slept. I awoke with a start and looked into the eyes of my tormentor. I tried to pull away, but the pain in my ankle seared through me and I gasped with pain. 'Try to rest, little songbird,' he lulled. 'We have a long way to go and I have patience but not complete tolerance when you will not do as I ask.'

"I looked at him in anger. 'How dare you speak to me like that! I am not your servant, and I know as soon as you can you will rid yourself of me!'

"He looked down at me and smiled. 'I have every right, as I am your new employer. As soon as that ankle is seen to I want you singing for the gentlemen in my best club.'

"'So you really want to employ me?' I looked at him, bewildered.

"'Yes,' he said, 'my little songbird. You are going on to a life of luxury, but for now settle down in my arms and sleep.' I smiled for the first time that day and trustingly, still quite naïve, I slept.

"Gentle hands helped me down and carried me in through a doorway that was splendid in marble and oak. I thought I must have still been dreaming as I was undressed, washed, and put into a small bed with a silky eiderdown comforter and soft, cool white sheets. I slept for so long and then remember a doctor giving me a sleeping pill and strapping up my badly bruised and sprained ankle. He told someone that I must rest in bed for at least two weeks and then rest in a chair for a further two weeks without putting any strain on my leg. I drifted in and out of sleep, feeling happy and then sad when I realized how I had gotten there. I woke up feverish, having dreamed of Daniel Blackman's tanned slim hands caressing me and making me feel so good—when I should have been feeling bad and ashamed. Eventually I was awake and well enough to sit out with my poor injured foot bathed and bandaged and placed on a footstool.

"Daniel Blackman was a very attentive host and my every wish was catered for. I only had to say how I loved the smell of roses before dozens of them picked from his garden would appear on my dressing room table. It felt good, all of this pampering, and day by day I grew to enjoy his company more and more. We would talk and laugh and eventually I fell for this smiling gentle man. I knew I was out of his league, but somehow love knew no boundaries. We soon became lovers and I moved into the main bedroom with him.

"I didn't feel that this was wrong and I knew that I could never be his wife, but I had all I needed and was soon the star attraction in his gentlemen's club. I saw lots of very pretty girls sitting and chatting to the gentlemen, but I had no idea that this was actually a high-class brothel—that was until a gentleman was thrown out with his trousers around his ankles for not paying his girl hostess.

"I felt sorry for the gentleman and disgusted by the circumstances. I approached my lover and asked him what kind of establishment he owned. He laughed at my coyness and reached forward, cradling one of my bosoms, and whispered, 'Why, my sweet? Do you think you are the only girl that can pleasure a man?' I felt humiliated and realized that I was no better than the prostitutes that took their gentlemen upstairs. I was still not sure all of the things this man who I loved and despised from moment to moment was into. I soon realized he was into gambling, prostitution, gun-running, and perhaps murder!

"The day I realized that I was as much involved in these things as he was came soon after. I was asked to look after a poor, frightened little boy. He was about three years old, well fed, and dressed very smartly in expensive clothes. I was told his name was Harry and asked never to leave his side but to look after him well, as he was Daniel's sister's child and she had died. We were to be looking after Harry until the family was able to find him a new home. My heart went out to this child and I tended him as if he were my own. He didn't answer me the first few times I spoke his name. He was not a bad tempered child but looked at me in confusion sometimes. He seemed to have a strange accent when he did speak. He was very polite. One of the girls that worked in the club had once told me she was from London, England, and although Harry had a posh voice, hers, although a bit guttural, was quite pleasant and similar. I wondered perhaps if Daniel's brother-in-law was English.

"Harry was such a sweet child, but during this time I never saw anyone, not even Daniel. I thought this was very strange. It was as if I had some sort of disease and was to be left alone. My meals were placed outside of my door. There was always just one meal, and I shared it with Harry. Even though he was not a big eater, it somehow did not seem right. Harry had only the clothes he was standing up in and a few pieces of new underwear that Daniel had brought that first day. As I said, I was completely isolated with this small, unhappy child. He would look at me sometimes with his huge eyes and say, 'Where are my mama and poppa?' My heart went out to this scrap of life. How could I tell him his mama was dead and his family was so distraught that they couldn't even visit him, and he was here with a stranger looking after him.

"Days went by, and being isolated, I didn't have as much as a newspaper or gossip from the club or anything to tell me even what day it was. Then the worst day of my life came.

"Daniel, who I had not seen for a fortnight or more, came bursting into the room in the early hours, looking like thunder. Both Harry and I awoke with a start and Harry started to cry softly. 'Whatever is wrong?' I cried, my eyes trying to search his face in the dimness of the room.

"'It's that,' he snarled, pointing at the now frightened little boy. I was shaken to the core.

"'How can you call your nephew that?' I cried, hardly

able to believe my own ears.

"Daniel sneered at me, 'My God, but you are so stupid,' he said, a sneer crossing his angry face. 'He isn't my nephew; he is Lord and Lady Monteg Smithe's only child. I would have thought that they would have given me at least a few thousand dollars for its safe return.'

"I could not believe what I was hearing! *It must be a nightmare*, I thought, but this was real hard and cold. I looked at Daniel in horror. 'What on earth are you talking about?" I shouted, my head and heart pounding so hard, in disbelief and terror now.

"'Come on!' Daniel snarled. 'Pull yourself together. We have got to get rid of the brat once and for all!' He brandished a gun and held it to the now terrified child's head. I don't know what happened next, but I was told that I flew across the room and snatched the child from his hands and held him close. I then heard a loud bang and everything went red and very peaceful. I do not remember anything else until I awoke and was told that after the shot, all hell broke loose. Police and gangsters were battling right outside of the room and when they eventually broke in, there was Daniel clutching me to him crying, 'What have I done to my little songbird?' The child was quickly removed and was taken safely back to his distraught parents. Daniel went quietly off to be held in custody, and was later sentenced to death."

A Step into Darkness

Melody wrapped her arms around the other girl and whispered, "None of this was your doing. You saved that little boy's life."

Both girls wept on each other's shoulders and eventually slept on top of one of the beds, their arms wrapped around each other as if keeping the pain between them.

The next morning was bright and clear. The warm sunshine warmed their backs and brightened their thoughts.

"Today is the first day of our task," Dorinda said as she smiled at the other girl as they light-heartedly ran toward the shores of the river.

The river was deep and murky between the two shores. On the girls' side there was smooth sand and waves gently touching the shore and, in contrast, sharp rocks stood on the other near the Shadow Land as huge waves battered the shore.

It looked very frightening. Much care was needed to cross, even at a point of the river that was slightly less swollen and dark. As they approached, a boatman was ready and waiting to get them on board. He was only able to cross at a certain time and was rushing the girls on without a greeting to set off across the mountainous waves. The boatman was very skilled at his craft as he pulled the boat this way and that. The girls were clinging to each other as the belts that the boatman insisted they wore to anchor them to the boat cut into their delicate skin, bruising and scraping them as the boat tossed high upon the tide, and then low as if the river was dragging them down hungrily into the pit of its stomach.

The girls, white with fear, turned frightened faces to one another and prayed that this part of their journey would soon be over. "Hold on tight!" shouted the boatman as a swell nearly capsized the boat, leaving it spinning dangerously near the ragged line of sharp rocks.

At last they were near the shore. The boatman unstrapped the girls and, as quick as he could, pushed them over the side of the boat and onto the dangerous, craggy rocks that looked like evil dark shapes in the water. "Go right ahead!" he shouted above the roar of the murky black water. "You will be safe. I cannot stop or I will be doomed to the Shadow Lands without my boat."

With those words he was tugged under the fierce waves, to pop back up coughing and spluttering a distance away. The girls made slow progress, dragging their wet cloaks behind them as they stumbled forward one slow step after another, until at last they reached the cold, austere foreshore of the Shadow Lands.

As soon as they stepped over the boundary line and into the Shadow Lands, the terrain went from smooth and bright to dark, foggy, and cold. Rocks, boulders, prickly plants, and deformed trees hampered their passage.

Although there was no pain or discomfort on the Light Planes, there was in this cold and forbidding place. This slowed their progress, and the smell of no drainage, rotting plants, and human suffering invaded their senses and made them urge with its repugnance. They needed to rest quite often and refresh their flagging spirits and tired bodies. They slept in the deformed trees as high as they could climb, making sure that they faded into the background and were not seen by anybody nearby.

They slept a while only to be awakened by the howl of a woman screaming as her husband beat her. Both girls were frightened but afraid to move in case the motion disturbed their robes and let out their light. Unable to help for fear of being discovered and with sickened hearts, the girls decided that as soon as this incident was over, they would move on. Soon the sounds came no more and they carefully slipped down the rotting branches of the tree to the prickly plants below and sharp stones all around.

Once down safely, the girls followed the pathway they were given. Although the terrain was tough, the girls kept on going. Now and again they heard the cries of suffering humanity, which tugged at their heartstrings and also filled them with dread and terror depending on how close the sounds were. Every tangle of reeds or sharp thorn caused them pain and frustration. Tree roots were everywhere in the dismal half light looking like grotesque creatures creeping across the ground, with their sharp or bulbous joints like elbows, knees, feet, and head. They could not escape from the stench of rot that filled their nostrils and seemed to seep into their very beings. After the first few gagging hours the girls grew more used to it, though they were glad that they at least would escape from it.

When they grew too weary to go on, they slept in trees, their cloaks covering them completely so no passing dark one would be able see them in the wizened tree, if they could be bothered to look up, that is. The dark ones were only looking for someone to rob, hurt, or jeer at. Occasionally the dark ones would get as far as the river and now and again would get a glimpse of the shore beyond. Few had tried to escape across the river only to find themselves thrown back by the first rolling wave that crashed them back onto the cold, sharp rocks again. It seemed to them they were never to escape this cruel, remorseless place, until they grew "soft," as the older ones put it.

Amongst some of the dark ones there were people who had talent in the arts, artists who painted landscapes of this grotesque place in dull grays, browns, and black, making the pictures even worse without a tiny glimpse of color. There were also some creatures with beautiful voices who were afraid to sing in case it gave his or her hiding place away and brought marauding gangs to terrorize them, smashing the small pieces of possessions they had brought with them into this soulless place, and stealing whatever was of any good to them. Children grew equally as evil as the insensitive adults, breaking every rule that governs a democratic society.

The girls had to work fast before the boy they had come to bring across the river and reunite with his family grew like these poor, lost children.

At last they reached the trees beside one of the foulest smelling stagnant pools of filthy water that the girls had ever seen. The report had come back to the light ones that a small boy, aged about seven, had just arrived with his feckless parents. He had been seen with a small piece of wood that he was trying to float in this foul water and mud. This tree was Jimmy's place at last. Both girls sat under the trees and waited long hours to see the child. The chilly, unending wind drew the evil smells to their nostrils and invaded their clothes, hair, and skin. So repugnant was it.

They took turns watching and sleeping, and then just as they were about to give up, a small head was seen close to the center of the foul-smelling pool.

Jimmy hated the life and place he was now in, but he thought that this would be his life forever now as his ma and pa had told him. "You, my boy, caused all this so don't start whining again or it will be the back of my hand you will be feeling!" This always came with a hard smack from one of them. He was glad to escape to the foul-smelling water just to be away from their continual nastiness to each other, or worse, to him.

He tried hard to remember how life was before coming here. The memories were failing the longer he stayed here, and he wanted to remember at least some good times. He cried when his mind played tricks on him and he thought he was born here, but he knew that was only his imagination.

The girls reached out with their hearts to the poor, young boy, so distressed and so young, trying desperately to float his wooden boat. He swore profoundly and slashed at the foul-smelling water with his boat. With each slash he became more and more uptight.

"I hate this place!" he screamed so loud it even disturbed the wind around him.

Melody opened her cloak a tiny amount and let out a little bit of her light. Right away, Jimmy backed away, frightened and very wary.

"Go away!" he shouted. "My pa is only over there and he has got weapons," he threatened. "Get away, you evil bright ones! You have only come to laugh and make us feel worse!"

he screeched.

Melody quickly closed her cloak and the two girls moved back a little, still watchful and sending out love.

Jimmy screeched until he was hoarse from screeching, and eventually his screeching turned to sobbing. He stood lost and alone, staring at the spot from which he had seen the light.

"Why have you come to make me feel even worse? I hate you!" he sobbed and threw soil at the broken trees. "Leave me alone; I don't want you here!" he yelled. He slumped forward into the smelly, filthy water and sat with the swamp up to his poor chest and swore.

His mother, disturbed by all his noise, called out from their hovel. "Shut yer roaring, ya little monster, or yer pa'll be out to give ya sumpin' to roar about. Now go somewhere, ya hear me? Ya good fer nuffin little sod!"

Jimmy thought, *Me hear her all right. I bet they can hear her in 'Stralia, wherever that is.*

He missed his friends and his balbies, especially his scarcies. He knew they were in his friends' pockets, but now that was unimportant to him. If he only could have his friends to play and laugh with. If only he wasn't here with his horrible parents. And now that light ones had come to mock him. How or why he hated them, he wasn't sure, but every time he had seem any of them, dark ones like him threw mud at them or tried to hurt them so he believed they must have been evil.

He got up suddenly, dashed out of the swamp, and disappeared into the murkiness, running as fast as his skinny, dirty legs would take him.

Dorinda sighed, "We will have to help him soon, poor little chap. He is going crazy here."

Melody looked at her friend in distress. "I know, but how will we reach him?"

They sat and waited and watched. They saw his mother occasionally look out over the swamp to see where her boy was, but she sighed with relief when she didn't see him. This made the girls feel even worse.

"How could his mother not be concerned about the poor little boy who was obviously so upset and alone in this frightening world where he didn't belong?" Dorinda sighed while Melody looked on sadly. They watched and waited, getting more and more anxious for his safety.

Dorinda smiled with pleasure as she thought of a beautiful little white lily. As she thought about it, one sprang up at the edge of the swamp! It was so beautiful that it looked so alien in this dark, dreary world. Melody smiled at Dorinda for her lovely present for Jimmy and was sure he would love it and want to see more.

Jimmy, not so far away, had been watching the two strangers. He knew there was two of them for now and when their cloaks would open just a little, he would have a glimpse of their beauty. He tried hard to hate them but was intrigued by them. He saw the taller of these ladies swish her cloak and saw her beautiful face. It looked soft and white, and he loved it when she smiled and a flower grew. Somehow he knew it was for him and was happier than he had been for ages.

He silently crept closer to the swamp and eventually stopped in front of the beautiful lily and just stared at it. It was so fair and beautiful with its lovely white flower and green leaves that it made him feel happy. He had not felt happy for so long. He remembered when his friend Johnny had stolen the dog's scruffy bone and had gotten a bite on the behind for his troubles. Jimmy laughed to himself, another thing he had forgotten how to do, and it felt strange to his ears as he heard it.

The girls, seeing his joy, came forward with delight, forgetting to shield their light in their pleasure. The sight of both of these clean, bright, and light young women startled Jimmy, who shouted and screeched at them in terror.

"Get away from me, ya evil, evil things!" he snarled like the wild animal he had become. "Get away!" he yelled, and started to throw the filth at them as he had seen countless others do while he was living in this hell hole.

He turned around and saw the beautiful lily. In his frenzy, he had covered it with the same filth he tried to cover the girls with. It slowly disappeared, and nothing was left where the flower had been except the gray, sludgy mud and evil smell.

"I hate you!" he screamed. "Why are you hurting me?"

Dorinda and Melody, shocked and saddened by his fear and hatred, pulled back and hid their light again. They sobbed as they realized how stupid they had been to scare him so. They still watched as Jimmy's shoulders slumped forward and he walked slowly away from them, picking up broken branches and slapping them against any old snarled tree he could find. Cursing and shouting abuse at them, he disappeared again into the fog.

For several days the girls waited and watched, careful not to be seen again. Eventually, a sad, frightened boy crawled into the swamp again and looked for his lily. It was nowhere to be seen. The girls, who were close by, stayed completely still, watching as the child searched the edge of the swamp for his beautiful present. He stopped looking as he unearthed a very sad, gray flower. He cried as he realized what he had done.

He sobbed and sobbed, heartbroken, and as his tears ran down his cheeks they splashed onto the lily. Slowly, the grayness turned white and green, for as Jimmy cried, the tears cleansed the flower. He opened his eyes and, as though in a trance, reached out and touched the tenderness of his beautiful flower. He sat next to the flower.

The girls slowly approached the boy and, without revealing themselves, allowed a tiny amount of light to show. Jimmy, not sure what to say or do or whether to run away again or stay and talk to these ladies who had given him this lovely gift, lifted his eyes. He decided if this flower was beautiful and felt so soft and lovely then these beautiful ladies could not wish him harm.

He looked up at the light and slowly said, "Hello."

Both girls sighed in delight as they uncovered just a little more at a time until their faces and eventually their clothes and shoes were uncovered in all their brightness and color.

Jimmy looked at the two young women in awe. "Who are ya?" he asked.

Both girls answered his questions and told him how they had been chosen to bring him into the light. He smiled at the girls and asked, "Who is going to look after me? Cuz, please, I don't want me ma or pa going with me,"

Melody explained, "Your mother and father need time away from you. They need to miss you and remember how to love you. Until then, they have to stay behind. Eventually, with your help, they will join you when they have learned to love and live together."

Jimmy looked satisfied with this explanation and got ready to go with the girls. He stopped in his tracks and said,

"Look at me; I'm filthy. How can I go with ya looking like this?" He sighed.

Dorinda smiled. She said, "Jimmy, look down at yourself."

He looked at his hands and saw that they were clean. He looked down at his feet and saw that he wore sandals. His legs, including his knees, were clean and bright. He was wearing blue shorts and a clean, white short-sleeved shirt. He looked at the girls in amazement. "How?" he asked.

Melody smiled at him. "When you cried, not only did those tears cleanse the lily, but your body and clothes as well."

"Wow!" He looked at his hands as if he hadn't seen them before. "I did this. Does this mean I can do magic?"

Both girls laughed. "You bet you can," said Dorinda, laughing aloud. "But for now let's get you home."

"Wait," said Jimmy. "Please, can we wait a minute?"

He rushed back to the edge of the swamp, reached forward, and pulled the lily with him.

Lightning Source UK Ltd.
Milton Keynes UK
UKOW051934271011

181063UK00001B/34/P